Dear mouse friends,
Welcome to the world of

Geronimo Stilton

THE RODENT'S GAZETTE
EDITORIAL STAFF

Geronimo Stilton
A learned and brainy
mouse; editor of
The Rodent's Gazette

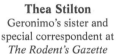

Thea Stilton
Geronimo's sister and
special correspondent at
The Rodent's Gazette

Trap Stilton
An awful joker;
Geronimo's cousin and
owner of the store
Cheap Junk for Less

Benjamin Stilton
A sweet and loving
nine-year-old mouse;
Geronimo's favorite
nephew

Geronimo Stilton

GERONIMO AND THE GOLD MEDAL MYSTERY

Scholastic Inc.

New York   Toronto   London   Auckland   Sydney

Mexico City   New Delhi   Hong Kong   Buenos Aires

ISBN-13: 978-0-545-02133-3
ISBN-10: 0-545-02133-2

Text by Geronimo Stilton
Original title *Lo strano caso dei Giochi Olimpici*
Cover by Cinzia Marrese and Daria Cerchi
Illustrations by Cinzia Marrese, Vittoria Termini, and Silvia Bigolin
Graphics by Zeppola Zap and Daniela Bossi

Special thanks to Beth Dunfey
Special thanks to Lidia Morson Tramontozzi
Interior design by Kay Petronio

12 11 10 9 8 7 6 5 4 3 2 1   8 9 10 11 12 13/0

Printed in the U.S.A.
First printing, April 2008

NOT THE OLYMPICS AGAIN!

It was a sweltering **HOT** summer morning. When my **ALARM WENT OFF**, I dragged my sorry tail out of bed and turned on the radio for the latest news.

"The **Olympics** are about to begin," the radio announcer **SHOUTED**. And I do mean **SHOUTED**.

I **ROLLED** my eyes. "Rat-munching rattlesnakes, the **Olympics**? That's all anyone in New Mouse City ever talks about! It's always **SPORTS, SPORTS, SPORTS**. Why doesn't anyone ever get **EXCITED** about the latest book on Neo-Ratonic

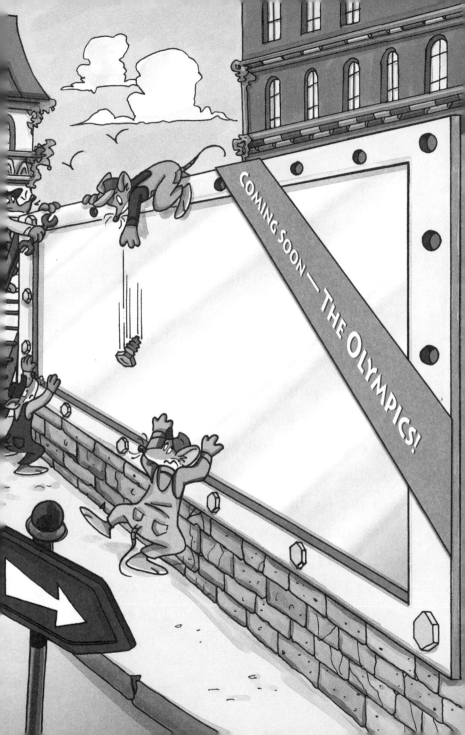

comparative philosophy?" I said with a SIGH.

I flipped through the newspaper and saw a huge headline:

ONLY THREE DAYS TO THE OLYMPICS!

"Moldy mozzarella, the **Olympics** again?" I snorted.

I left my mouse hole and headed for the office. And what was the first thing I saw? Workers putting up an **enormouse** TV screen right in the middle of town! Why? So everyone could watch the **Olympics** live, of course!

I got to the office and saw that everybody was abuzz. They were all talking about . . . the **Olympics**, of course!

So I locked myself in my *peaceful* office. You see, I am a bit of a bookmouse.

Oops, that reminds me — I almost forgot

to tell you! My name is Stilton, *Geronimo Stilton.* I'm the publisher and editor in chief of *The Rodent's Gazette,* the most popular newspaper on Mouse Island.

I was settled in reading a manuscript when suddenly, I heard the **roar** of a motor approaching. There was only one mouse I knew who would dare make that much noise in my nice, *quiet* office. . . .

Gerry Berry, I Need A Teensy-Weensy Favor...

A second later, the door **burst** open and my sister Thea, special correspondent to *The Rodent's Gazette,* made a grand entrance.

"Thea, how many times do I have to tell you not to ride your motorcycle into my office?" I GROANED.

My sister ignored me. She went right ahead and parked her bike on top of my desk. In the process, she squished my tail, FLATTENED my paw, and stained my favorite jacket with motor oil!

Before I could squeak in protest, she bent down and whispered sweetly in my ear, "Little brother! I brought you your favorite cheese

puffs from the bakery. You know, the ones with **blue cheese** stuffing and Parmesan sprinkled on top?"

Mmmm . . . that *did* sound delicious. But I was wary. When my sister acts nice, it's usually because she has something up her fur!

"Gerry Berry, I need to ask you an itsy-bitsy, teensy-weensy little favor," Thea continued.

I smiled. I know my sister like a cat knows its claws. And even though she drives me crazy, I'd do anything for her. "Sure. What is it?"

"I need you to cover the **Olympics**," she BLURTED out.

I was stunned. "B-b-but . . . I thought Grandfather asked you to cover it." Our grandfather William Shortpaws was the founder of *The Rodent's Gazette*. He ruled with an iron paw.

"Yes, but something came up.

Besides, you're such a **fine** rodent . . . so **intelligent**, so **professional**, so on **top of things**. . . ."

"Forget it! I know SQUAT about sports!" I objected.

Thea just *smiled* at me. "But you've got to go! It's been decided! Even Grandfather said so!"

As if on cue, the phone **RANG**. I picked it up at once. "Hello, Stilton here. *Geronimo Stilton*!"

A voice **thundered** in my ear so loudly, my eardrums almost **shattered**.

"Shortpaws here, **WILLIAM SHORTPAWS**!"

I SIGHED deeply.

Before I knew it, Grandfather started barking orders at me. "Grandson, listen up:

1. **RUN** home and pack your suitcase.

2. **GO STRAIGHT** to the airport.

3. **TAKE THE FIRST FLIGHT** to Athens!

"You're going to cover the **Olympics**! **FIRST**, I want you to write a juicy article for *The Rodent's Gazette*. **THEN**, I'll need you to do a daily live TV broadcast. And **FINALLY**, since you'll already be there, make sure to pick me up some Greek cheese!"

I tried to reason with him. "B-b-but, Grandfather, I'm busy. . . ."

"Don't argue with your grandfather!" he thundered.

What could I do? Thea has always had Grandfather *wrapped* around her little paw. And, of course, there's no arguing with Grandfather once he's made up his mind.

There was nothing to do but scamper home, pack my suitcase, and get to the airport as *fast* as my paws could carry me.

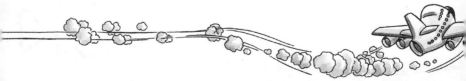

ATHENS

SPARTA

CRETE

GREECE

Area: 50,942 square miles
Population: 10.7 million
Language: Greek
Currency: Euro
Capital: Athens
Borders: Albania, Macedonia, and
Bulgaria to the north; Turkey to
the east. Greece is a peninsula
surrounded by water on three sides.
It is flanked by the Ionic Sea on the
west; the Aegean Sea on the east; and
the Mediterranean Sea on the south.

I Am A True
Gentlemouse...

Ooooooooh!

I boarded the plane to Athens and started looking for my seat. As soon as I had settled in, I heard a high-pitched squeak, "Ooooooooooooooh...."

I turned and saw a flight attendant with a **velvety fur** coat, a slender snout, and powdered whiskers. She had fake eyelashes, bright **red** lipstick, and looooooooooooong polished nails. Her **CROOKED** little paws were squeezed inside yellow spiked high heels.

I noticed she had just dropped her handkerchief. Being a gentlemouse, I got up and ran to retrieve it. I bowed, *kissed her paw*, and gave it back to her.

"**Ooooh**! You are a true gentlemouse!" she squeaked.

Then she accidentally **dropped** a small suitcase on my right paw!

"**OOOOOOOOOOUCH!**"

Aaaaah!

I screamed. But I wasn't about to let a little excruciating pain get in the way of my good manners. So I reached down to pick up the suitcase. Then I bowed, *kissed her paw*, and gave it back to her.

"At your service, madam," I said.

At that moment, she **dropped** an **ENORMOUSE** suitcase on my left paw!

"**YOOOWWWZAH!**" I screeched. But I still managed to reach down, pick up the heavy suitcase, return it to her, bow, and *kiss her paw.* "Still at your service, madam," I gasped.

The flight attendant ducked her head modestly. "Oh, you are such a *polite* mouse! Would you mind helping me show the movie?"

Moments later, I was wrestling with a mountain of filmstrips that had wound themselves around my neck like snakes.

"I'm **SUFFOCAAAAAATING!**" I hissed desperately.

As soon as I had untangled the tape, I bowed to the flight attendant and *kissed her paw.* "Still at your service, madam!" I gasped.

She *smiled sweetly* at me. "Oh, you are such a sweet mouse! Would you mind helping me **clean** all the restrooms on the plane?"

I had no choice but to clean those foul-smelling plane restrooms. The stench was enough to knock a sewer rat unconscious! When I finished, I gave the flight attendant back the pail and brush.

She gave me her *sweetest* smile yet. "Oh, you are such a knowledgeable mouse! Would you mind . . ."

Now I was TRULY worried. What else could she want me to do?! Fly the plane? I am a very nervous mouse, you know. . . .

So I asked veeeeeery cautiously, "How else may I help you, madam?"

It was then that I took a closer look at the flight attendant and realized something EXTREMELY bizarre.

MY DEAR STILTON, DID YOU LIKE MY LITTLE JOKE?

The flight attendant had ... a banana peel peeking out of her pocket!

I peered at her. There was something familiar about that **long**, SLENDER snout and those CROOKED little paws. Could it be?

This was no flight attendant! It was my old friend HERCULE POIRAT, the private detective! He often traveled undercover in order to keep his investigations a SECRET. He truly was a master of disguise. Why, he'd fooled even me — and we've been friends since kindergarten!

Hercule whipped off his wig and false eyelashes. "My dear Stilton, did you like my little joke?" he asked, chuckling.

I tried to be a good sport — really, I did! But the memory of those restrooms was too much for me. "**NOOOOOOOOO!**" I shrieked. "I didn't find it funny at all!"

But Hercule had already forgotten about the dirty ~~tricks~~ he'd played on me. That was just like him. "You're going to the **Olympics**, right?" he asked in a low voice.

"Why, y-y-yes." I stammered, surprised. "Why do you ask?"

Before he answered, Hercule looked around to see if anyone was listening. "I'm going to the **Olympics**, too," he whispered at last. "Any idea why I'm going to the Olympics?"

"I don't have a clue," I told him. "And I'm not sure I want to know!" Hercule's investigations often led him into **DANGER** . . . and as you may know, I am a bit of a scaredy mouse!

"Well, I'm afraid I'm going to have to tell you anyway," he said. "Look, something **rotten** is going on at the **Olympic Games**. I could really use your help, old friend."

"Sorry, but I can't help this time, Hercule," I said. "I'm going to Athens to write a **SPECIAL REPORT** on the **Olympics** for *The Rodent's Gazette*. My grandfather has me snout-deep in work all week long."

Hercule didn't seem to have heard me. "By the way, where's Thea?" he asked.

"She couldn't come, **unfortunately**. Grandfather has her on another assignment."

Hercule groaned loudly — so loudly that

everyone on the plane turned to stare at us.

"WHAAAAAAAAAAAT? My adorable Thea isn't here?" He started sobbing.

I was very embarrassed. "Shhh, please lower your voice. Everybody is staring at us!"

"And to think I was all set to propose to her in Athens!" he lamented, holding his snout in his paws. "I even bought her an ENGAGEMENT RING."

I tried not to roll my eyes. "You can ask her another time."

Hercule dried his tears. "I'll concentrate on my work. That's what I'll do. I'll try to distract myself by solving this **Olympics** mystery. That'll keep my mind off Thea. Come on, Stilton, don't be such a fly in the fondue. You know, this case could give you some great headlines for your newspaper."

"I've already told you, I'm booked solid! I really can't help you," I protested.

Hercule burst into tears again.

"Oh, don't start that again!" I begged him. He kept on sobbing.

Finally, I gave in. What else could I do? I am a **soft-hearted** mouse. "Okay, fine, stop sniffling. What's the case all about?"

Instantly, he was all smiles. "Take a look at the list of all the countries participating in the **Olympics**. Soon you'll understand." He glanced at his watch. "I've got to go. I have to serve a **CHEESE SNACK** to the passengers." He paused for a moment, as if he'd just had an idea. "By the way, my *dear* Stilton, since you're so kind, would you help me?"

A LITTLE CONFESSION

I have a confession to make, dear reader. I didn't want to let on in front of Hercule Poirat, but I was actually pretty intrigued by his case.

As soon as I got off the plane, I hooked up my laptop, went ONLINE, and checked out the list of countries participating in the **Olympics**.

But I didn't notice anything funny about it.

COUNTRIES PARTICIPATING IN THE ATHENS OLYMPICS

Afghanistan

Albania

Algeria

American Samoa

Andorra

Angola

Antigua and Barbuda

Argentina

Armenia

Aruba

Australia

Austria

Azerbaijan

The Bahamas

Bahrain

Bangladesh

Barbados

Belarus

Belgium

Belize

Benin

Bermuda

Bhutan

Bolivia

Bosnia and
Herzegovina

Botswana

Brazil

British Virgin
Islands

Brunei

Bulgaria

Burkina Faso

Burundi

Cambodia

Cameroon

Canada

Cape Verde

Cayman Islands

Central African
Republic

Chad

Chile

China

Colombia

Comoros

Congo, Democratic
Republic of the

Congo,
Republic of the

Cook Islands

Costa Rica

Croatia

Cuba

Cyprus

Czech Republic

Denmark

Djibouti

Dominica

Dominican
Republic

East Timor

Ecuador

Egypt

El Salvador

Equatorial
Guinea

Eritrea

 Estonia

Ethiopia

 Fiji

Finland

France

Gabon

Gambia

Georgia

Germany

Ghana

 Great Britain

Greece

Grenada

Guam

Guatemala

Guinea

Guinea-Bissau

Guyana

Haiti

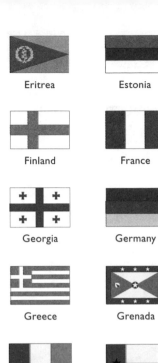 Honduras

Hong Kong

Hungary

 Iceland

 India

Indonesia

Iran

 Iraq

 Ireland

Israel

Italy

 Ivory Coast

 Jamaica

 Japan

 Jordan

 Kazakhstan

Kenya

Kiribati

Kuwait

Kyrgyzstan

Laos

Latvia

Lebanon

Lesotho

Liberia

Libya

Liechtenstein

Lithuania

Luxembourg

Macedonia

Madagascar

Malawi

Malaysia

Maldives

Mali

Malta

Mauritania

Mauritius

Mexico

Micronesia

Moldavia

Monaco

Mongolia

Morocco

Mozambique

Myanmar

Namibia

Nauru

Nepal

Netherlands

Netherlands
Antilles

New Zealand

Nicaragua

Niger

Nigeria

North Korea

Norway

Oman

Pakistan

Palau

Palestine

Panama

Papua
New Guinea

Paraguay

Peru

Philippines

Poland

Portugal

Puerto Rico

Qatar

Romania

Russia

Rwanda

Saint Kitts
and Nevis

Saint Lucia

Saint Vincent and
the Grenadines

Samoa

San Marino

São Tomé and
Principe

Saudi Arabia

Senegal

Serbia and
Montenegro

Seychelles

Sierra Leone

Singapore

Slovakia

Slovenia

Solomon Islands

Somalia

South Africa

South Korea

Spain

Sri Lanka

Sudan

Suriname

Swaziland

Sweden

Switzerland

Syria

Taiwan

Tajikistan

Tanzania

Thailand

Togo

Tonga

Trinidad and
Tobago

Tunisia

Turkey

Turkmenistan

Uganda

Ukraine

United Arab
Emirates

United States

Urugauy

Uzbekistan

Vanuatu

Venezuela

Vietnam

Yemen

Zambia

Zimbabwe

DURING
ANCIENT TIMES

I had a zillion things to do for Grandfather. But no trip to Athens would be complete without a little sightseeing!

Athens is truly MARVeLºUS. Our first stop was the Parthenon, an ancient temple dedicated to the goddess Athena, the protector of the city. Holey cheese, it was spectacular!

That night, I went out to dinner. My guidebook had lots of recommendations for restaurants that specialized in LOCAL CHEESES.

The following MORNING, I went to **Mouse TV's** headquarters in **Athens**.

The Parthenon was built between 447 and 432 B.C. on the Acropolis (which in ancient Greek means "high city") in Athens. It is one of the most famous monuments in the world. The temple's interior chamber held a statue of Athena dressed in gold. There were marble sculptures outside the temple that were painted in very bright colors. Today, many of the columns and statues from the original Parthenon can be seen at the British Museum in London.

THE ANCIENT GREEKS

Around 1000 B.C., independent city-states began to form in Greece. (The term city-state is used to describe large cities and the villages that surrounded them.) The most famous were the rival city-states of Athens and Sparta. In the fifth century B.C., Greek city-states spread throughout the Mediterranean. Several of these city-states organized themselves into a loose union. Their growing power led to war against the Persians, who lived in what is today the Middle East. The Greeks defeated the Persians at the battles of Marathon, Salamis, and Plataea.

SPARTAN WARRIORS *underwent extremely rigorous military discipline and athletic training. At the age of seven, they began preparing themselves for all sorts of hardship.*

The military and political prestige of Athens grew during the Age of Pericles (450–429 B.C.) and rekindled the rivalry between Sparta and Athens. The Peloponnesian War (431–404 B.C.) signaled the decline of Athens and the prominence of Sparta. With Philip II of Macedonia in charge, Greece lost its independence. In 146 B.C., it became a province of the Roman Empire.

HOMER

Homer was a blind poet who lived between the seventh and eighth century B.C. He is said to be the author of two very famous epic poems, **The Iliad** *and* **The Odyssey**. *The Iliad recalls the war with Troy, a city-state in present-day Turkey. The Odyssey describes the adventures of the Greek warrior Ulysses on his voyage home to Ithaca from Troy.*

EDUCATION

In ancient Greece, education, which was reserved only for males, began when a child was around seven years old. Several subjects were taught: reading, writing, gymnastics, and music. Then boys learned how to recite poetry. Very little time was spent on math. Girls stayed home and were taught by their mothers to weave, cook, and sing.

FOOD

Wheat and barley were the most cultivated grains in ancient Greece. They were used to make bread. Olive trees and grape vines were also important crops. Olive oil was used for cooking and also in medicine and cosmetics. Grapes were eaten as fruit or pressed to make wine. Cheese and fish were also staples of the Greek diet. Only chickens and pigs were raised for meat. Sheep and goats were used for their milk, wool, and skin. Cows and mules worked in the fields. Honey was used as a sweetener. Sugar had not yet been discovered.

THE GAMES IN OLYMPIA

The Greek city-states were always fighting amongst themselves. Only on special occasions were they at peace with one another. But every four years, a truce was called for the athletic games held in honor of the god Zeus in the city of Olympia. It was from this event that the modern-day Olympics takes its name.

The games probably began around 776 b.c. They were held every four years for approximately twelve hundred years, until the Romans conquered Greece. One reason for the games' demise was that they were of pagan origin, and the Roman Empire was slowly shifting toward Christianity.

WHO PARTICIPATED?

City-states sent their best athletes to compete against one another in the Games. However, only men were allowed to participate. Women were absolutely prohibited even to attend! Women could not officially participate in the Games until many centuries later, in 1900.

HOW THE GAMES WERE ANNOUNCED

Games were announced by torchbearers. Athletes holding torches ran through Greece to announce the opening of the games. This tradition continues today, with the lighting of the Olympic flame at the beginning of each games.

...IN HONOR OF ZEUS

What Games Were Played?

Spectators enjoyed watching all the track and field competitions and the pentathlon, which included five events — running, long jump, discus, javelin, and wrestling. The chariot and horse races were also crowd favorites. Fans particularly enjoyed combat sports (not surprising, since the ancient gods were always fighting!), especially the pancratium, a mixture of wrestling and boxing in which a little of everything was permitted: punching, biting, and slapping until one of the two athletes surrendered.

To The Victor

A crown of olive leaves, taken from trees that grew near the temple dedicated to Zeus, was awarded to the winner of each competition.

The athletes rubbed their skin with olive oil to warm up their muscles. To make their bodies less slippery, and to get a stronger grip, they sprinkled sand on themselves.

IT'S NOT MY FAULT
I'M SHY!

The cameramouse **Jack McZoomerson** greeted me at TV headquarters. He looked at me suspiciously. "Do you know anything about sports?"

"**Absolutely nothing!**" I admitted.

"Do you know anything about TV reporting?" he demanded.

"**Nope, not a thing,**" I confessed. "I'm a newspaper mouse."

"Ever tried talking on live TV?" he asked next.

"**Never!**" I said in complete honesty. He shook his snout in annoyance. After a moment, Jack took pity on me and gave me some advice. "Look,

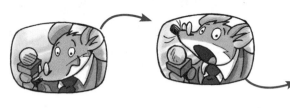

try to relax. Don't let anyone see that you're **SCARED** out of your wits, that you have no idea what you're doing, that you're about to make a fool of yourself, that you know diddly about sports."

I hardly realized it, but I must've let out a SQUEAK OF FRIGHT.

"Oh, don't start whimpering now!" Jack shouted at me. "How about if we have a little rehearsal? Look at the camera, but don't **STARE**. Try to look SMART and funny.

"Ready? **One, two, three . . . you're on!**"

I tried my best. Honestly, I did!

"Ahem, huh, good morning, my *Stilton* is name, that is, my last name is *Geronimo*. I'm here to talk to you

about . . . that is, the **Olympics** are over . . . no, that's not correct, they're about to begin here in **Thea** . . . that's my sister's name, you see . . . "

I burst into tears. "I'll never be able to do it! It's not my fault I'm *shy!*"

Jack tried to cheer me up. "Come on, it wasn't so bad. Why, with a little practice, you might be able to report on the weather. . . . "

He paused to give me a pitying look. "Anyway, I won't be the one filming. Your grandfather called to say that all the shooting will be done by . . ."

At that moment, the door swung open. A familiar snout peered through.

"Hello, old friend!" Then he turned to Jack. "The name's POIRAT, HERCULE POIRAT."

This was simply too much. I had to

protest. "Oh, no! If he is going to film me, I **REFUSE TO DO IT**!"

Hercule looked at me and *smiled*. "My dear Stilton, I have the very thing to cheer you up. Would you like a banana?"

"No! I don't want to eat any bananas!" I shouted.

Hercule just looked at me SADLY. Then he pulled out his cell phone. "Your grandfather would like a word with you."

This is how the conversation went.

"**Grandson,** squeak SQUEAK squeak SQUEAK...."

"Yes, Grandfather!"

"SQUEAK SQUEAK SQUEAK SQUEAK!"

"Yes, Grandfather. I understand!"

At the end of the conversation, I hung up with a sigh.

Sometimes you have to know when to throw in the cheesecloth.

LET THE GAMES BEGIN!

I **dreaded** the next day, but there was nothing I could do. So I took a deep breath and got ready for my first live broadcast: the opening ceremony of the **Olympics**!

An athlete carrying the Olympic FLAME entered the stadium at a *run*. He looked downright pooped. But as soon as he came in, the *fun* began! There was an **enormouse** parade. It was amazing to see mice from all over the world coming together.

AND THE
WINNER IS...

The next day, the Games began at last.

I was scampering around frantically, trying to broadcast from every competition.

First, there was the **WEIGHTLIFTING** competition. Crusty kitty litter, were those athletes **STRONG**! They could lift more than a thousand pounds. I'd never be able to do that! And the winner was . . . an athlete from a faraway country: *Mousylvania*!

Next, I *scampered* to the track and field stadium and began my report. I was in such a hurry, I didn't even have time to be nervous!

"Here at the **hundred-meter** dash, the athletes are about to start. They're *RUNNING* . . . they crossed the finish line in less than five seconds! The first to cross the finish line is an athlete from . . . Mousylvania!"

Then it was time for **pole-vaulting**.

"One after the other, the athletes start at a run. They're vaulting more than TWENTY-SEVEN FEET! And the winner comes from . . . Mousylvania!"

Hercule, who was next to me filming the competition, leaned over and asked, "My dear Stilton, would you like a banana?"

"No, thank you. I think I've mentioned that I

don't eat bananas!" I replied.

"Are you sure? Look, it's a delicious banana. Besides, it's good for you."

"NO, no, noooooooooooooo!! What do you want from me? I've told you at least a *MILLION TIMES*, I don't like bananas!"

"Touchy, touchy!" Hercule said.

Hercule whispered to me, "My dear Stilton, have you noticed anything a little . . . unusual . . . about the competitions?"

Now it was my turn to be surprised. "No, I can't say that I have."

The team games began next. All of the nations participated, except the team from Mousylvania.

I was stumped. What did Hercule mean?

Hercule shook his **snout** sadly. "They said you were the smart one, but I always knew better."

SOMETHING ROTTEN IN THE STATE OF MOUSYLVANIA

Hercule Poirat began to peel another banana. "My dear friend, I'm afraid the mold has started to grow over your cheese. There are **three** very unusual things that I noticed and that you did not," he said with a small smirk.

1. "If you look at the results of all the countries participating in the Olympics, there is one country that does not exist: Mousylvania!

2. All of Mousylvania's athletes look alike — too much alike!

3. Mousylvania has not participated in any team sports, only in individual competitions!

And that's because there is only one athlete representing the entire country!"

I was shocked. "Are you sure? I didn't notice a thing!"

Hercule nodded and leaned in close. "We've got to get into the **Olympic Village** . . . no ifs, ands, or buts! All the athletes are housed there. We must figure out what Mousylvania is up to! The village is well guarded, and the public is not allowed inside. But have no **FEAR**, Hercule Poirat is here! I've gotten my paws on a map of the village. Look, this is where Mousylvania is staying. I've also figured out some ways of getting in.

1. Dig a tunnel.

2. Dress like mail carriers and pretend we're delivering an express package.

3. Use a parachute.

4. Hide in the garbage truck.

OR...we COULD...we COULD...we COULD..."

His voice trailed off. He was clearly lost in thought, pondering how we could sneak into the Olympic Village.

"Or," I said with a laugh,

"we COULD uSe MY PReSS paSS."

We headed toward the Olympic Village gate. I showed my press card to the guard, and he let us in.

Hercule was impressed. "What a simple solution to a complex problem! My dear Stilton, I guess sometimes it takes a mouse of ordinary intelligence to see what the smartest rat in the room cannot."

I just grumbled. I don't know who is more annoying: my cousin Trap or Hercule Poirat!

IN THE DARK OF NIGHT...

We headed straight for the building where the team from Mousylvania was staying. We hid until **DARKNESS** fell. Then, quiet as mice, we snuck into the building.

We knew that if Mousylvania really had a team, their quarters would be crowded with athletes, coaches, trainers, and reporters. But instead, it was empty. There was no one there!

We decided to split up so we could cover more ground. I turned **RIGHT** and Hercule Poirat turned **LEFT**. As I looked around those large deserted rooms, my heart pounded so fast I

thought it would pop out of my chest! It was dark, and the only source of LIGHT was the teeny-tiny flashlight on my keychain.

In the **DARK**, those big, EMPTY rooms gave me the heebie-jeebies.

From behind a column, I heard a creepy voice yell, "**Yooo-hooo!**"

Who could it be? Before I could find out, I fainted from FRIGHT.

"Yoo-hoo, Stilton, come see . . . I mean, hear!"

When I came to, I realized it was only Hercule! It was just like him to scare the fur off of me. But I was relieved to see my friend, so I followed him. We tiptoed toward a solid **STONE** door that was cracked open. We could hear strange animal sounds, as if an entire zoo lay inside!

MEOW! *Roar!* *Ribbit!*

HOO! HOO! **Squak!**

ZZZZZZZZZZ...

Slowly, Hercule Poirat swung the door open. Before us was a **HUGE** room filled with cages and tanks holding every type of animal: ants, flies, grasshoppers, hummingbirds, frogs, rabbits, jaguars, apes, monkeys, elephants, dolphins.

What were these animals doing here? And what did they have to do with the **Olympics**?

In the middle of the room, there was an **enormouse** machine attached to two armchairs. An old rodent was chained to one of them. He was snoring loudly.

"**Zzzz...zzzzzz! Zzzzzzzz...zzzzzzzzz!**"

As we crept closer, I recognized him. "Why, it's my old friend **Professor Paws von Volt**!" I told Hercule. "About a year ago,

he disappeared MYSTERIOUSLY, and no one has heard anything from him since! It seemed that at the time he was conducting some EXTREMELY SECRET experiments in genetics."

We were about to wake him up when we heard a floorboard in the hallway squeak.

"Hurry, my dear Stilton!" cried Hercule. "Let's hide in that corner. And be quick about it!"

GENETICS is the science that deals with the hereditary characteristics of species in the plant and animal world.

THE END JUSTIFIES THE MEANS

We hid behind a row of cages and waited for the door to open.

A tall, thin, *very elegant-looking* rat entered the room. He had blond hair and blue eyes that were as cold as ice. His double-breasted jacket had a family crest embroidered with the words, *The end justifies the means!* But what really struck me was his CRUEL expression. He had the snout of a rodent without scruples or feelings.

He reminded me of someone . . . but who?

Then I got it!
He looked just

like the athletes from Mousylvania we had seen competing that morning!

I imagined him first with a **BEARD** and whiskers . . . then with different color hair . . . then with a pimple on the tip of his snout . . . **YES, YES, YES!** It was him. It was really him!

He stood over the professor with a triumphant look on his face. When my old friend didn't wake up, the cruel-looking mouse nudged him with his paw.

Professor von Volt woke with a **start**.

"Professor, I have won another GOLD MEDAL! Are you happy?"

The professor was indignant. "Happy, *von Snootrat*? No, I wouldn't say that. In fact, I'm disgusted! You didn't deserve that medal. You won it by cheating!"

Count Cyrus von Snootrat

Who he is: A rodent without feelings or morals. He's tall, thin, and extremely elegant. His eyes are blue and as cold as ice.

What he wants: To be the greatest athlete in the whole world.

What he wears: A double-breasted jacket with his family crest and motto embroidered on it: *The end justifies the means!*

His secret: He forced Professor von Volt to use the Voltometer on him so he could win all the Olympic competitions.

His dream: To become very, very rich and conquer Mouse Island.

His weak point: He does not know how to lose.

PROFESSOR VON VOLT'S SECRET

The count laughed and pointed to the crest on his *very elegant* jacket. "Do you see this crest with my family's motto? The end justifies the means!"

Before Professor von Volt could respond, *Cyrus von Snootrat's* cell phone rang.

"Yes? This is *Count von Snootrat*. With whom am I speaking? Oh, is that you, Nemo?"

As he spoke, the count began pumping huge **WEIGHTS**. Hercule Poirat and I exchanged glances. There was no way a skinny, weak-looking rat like him could lift those weights!

Then he continued his conversation. "Yes, thanks to the professor's **INGENIOUS**

MACHINE, it's possible to transfer any characteristics from one subject to another. That's how I've been able to win so many **Olympic** competitions!"

I could feel anger bubbling up inside of me. The other athletes at the Games had spent years training for the Olympics! And this horrible rodent had stolen the competitions right out from under them!

Meanwhile, *Count von Snootrat* was still boasting. "Yes, for pole-vaulting,

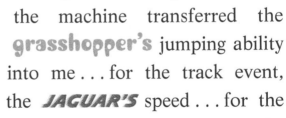

the machine transferred the **grasshopper's** jumping ability into me . . . for the track event, the **JAGUAR'S** speed . . . for the weightlifting competition, the strength of an **ant** . . . and the machine can also give me the *radar* of a bat . . . the ability to see in the **DARK** like a cat . . . the climbing skills of a monkey. . .

"Yes, the machine would certainly be considered a major scientific breakthrough if it were known to the public. But we'll just keep it to ourselves," he cackled. "Soon we'll have Mouse Island in the palm of our paws!"

He shut the phone and stroked his whiskers with a snobbish air.

I shivered. I wanted to leap out of our hiding spot and wrestle him to the ground. I may not be a strong mouse, but I was **STEAMING MAD**!

STRONG AS AN ANT, FAST AS A BUNNY

Cyrus von Snootrat stroked his whiskers. "Soon the **LONG** jump competition will start. And naturally, I will win it!"

He rummaged through the cages until he found one that held a frog.

"**Aha**, this is just what I need. A **frog**! No one can leap longer or higher than a frog. Professor, please see that my brain is immediately connected to the frog's."

Professor Paws von Volt did not move. "No, *Count von Snootrat*. I will not. I don't like these experiments on defenseless animals. I invented the **VOLTOMETER** for a

completely different reason: to help doctors fight incurable diseases. You have **FORCED** me to help you, but now I'm done. I refuse to be a part of your dishonest plan!"

Cyrus von Snootrat smirked. "Well, fortunately for me, I don't need your help anymore! I paid close attention to how this machine works and can do it myself!"

By now Hercule had had **ENOUGH**. "What a **TERRIBLE, TERRIBLE** rat! That's not playing fair. We need to turn him in **RIGHT AWAY**!" he whispered to me.

"But how?" I whispered back. "He's so **strong**! He could easily overpower the two of us."

Hercule gave a sly smile. He pulled out a small **DIGITAL CAMERA** from one of his many trench coat pockets. "We'll take pictures of everything! Then we'll have the **proof** we need to send that slimy sewer rat to jail. We'll wait until he leaves for the next competition, then we'll rescue your friend the professor, **SLIP** away, and bring the photos to the authorities."

I smiled admiringly. Hercule really was a good detective.

He raised the camera . . . and bumped a cage with his elbow!

A Breathtaking Tailchase

The cage fell on top of the cage in front of it, and that cage fell on top of the one in front of it,

AND THAT CAGE FELL ON TOP OF THE ONE IN FRONT OF IT, UNTIL SUDDENLY THERE WERE DOZENS OF CAGES FALLING, FALLING, FALLING . . .

Strangely, HERCULE didn't seem at all alarmed. "**OOPS**! What a mess I've made!" he giggled.

Count Cyrus von Snootrat turned . . . and saw us! "Who are you? What are your names? Where did you come from? How long have you been spying on me? Why are you here?"

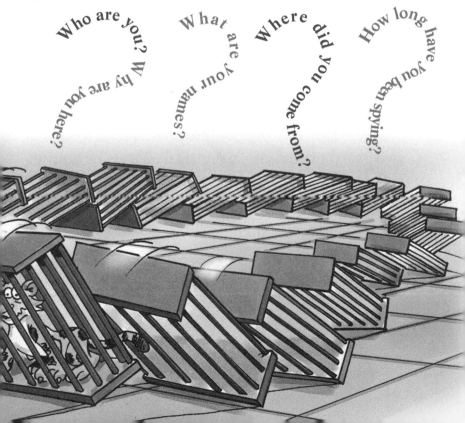

Hercule just stuck his tongue out at him. Then he began taking photos at supersonic speed.

Count von Snootrat shouted angrily, "Give me that camera NOW! Do you UNDERSTAAAAAAAND?"

With a swift leap (holey cheese, he really *was* fast!), he grabbed the detective by the tail. HERCULE tossed the camera to me.

"Catch it, Stilton! Catch it!"

I caught the camera on the fly. And the count was after me in an instant! A breathtaking tailchase around the lab had begun!

A LITTLE
SWITCHEROO

Cyrus von Snootrat laughed evilly. "Why am I even bothering to chase you? This amazing machine will help me catch up with you instantly. In mere seconds, I'll be able to run as *fast* as a bunny rabbit!"

With that, he **VAULTED** into the air and landed on the chair. As he leaped, he grabbed a frightened rabbit and switched on the **VOLTOMETER**. But he was so busy multitasking he didn't notice that **Professor Paws von Volt** had switched the bunny rabbit with another animal . . . a snail!

The machine began to hum as it warmed up.

Brrrrrrzzzz . . . brrrzzzzzz . . . brzzzzzzz . . .

When the buzzing stopped, *Cyrus von Snootrat* tried to get up, but his movements were very, veeeeeeeeery slooooooow . . . just like a **snail's**!

He opened his mouth to speak. We waited . . . and waited . . . and waited. Finally, he managed to say,

"R-R-R-R-R-A-A-A-A-A-T-T-T-S-S-S-S-S-S!"

I'll Pluck Your Whiskers!

I ran to Professor von Volt and freed him from his chains. Meanwhile, HERCULE POIRAT called the Athens **POLICE** on his cell phone.

"Hello? Is this the police? I've got a nasty little rat ready for handcuffs. . . . Can you come pick him up? . . . Is he dangerous? **NO**, not anymore. . . . He was speedy before, but now he's lost the spring in his step. Noooo. You might even say he's feeling a little **sluggish**."

HERCULE was right. *Cyrus von Snootrat* had become really slow. Half an hour later, when the police came to take him away, he was still trying to get up out of his chair!

The professor took pity on him and turned on the **VOLTOMETER**. With a hum, the machine gave him back his regular speed.

As soon as he could talk normally, *Cyrus von Snootrat* started screaming insults at us. His snout grew redder and redder with anger.

"**YOU SEWER RATS!** You low-grade class of RODENTS! Substandard species of **MICE**! If I catch you, I'll tie your tails together! I'll pluck off your whiskers!"

I'll pluck your whiskers....

"Oh, well, looky here!" Hercule laughed. "For such a snob, it doesn't take much to get your snout bent out of shape, does it? I can tell you're a big fat liar and not a real athlete because *you don't know how to looooose!*"

A true athlete knows how to accept defeat!

As Easy as Nibbling on Cheese!

I hugged **Professor Paws von Volt**. "I'm so happy to see you, Professor! Are you okay? Can you tell us how this **machine** works? I'm very curious."

My old friend laughed. "Why, it's as easy as nibbling on **cheese**! Let me explain. All you need to do is to calculate the cubic root of the Rattic formula of the demouseratto logarithm. Then factor in the geometric potassimeter micromouse of the centrifugal titaniumicic of the quanton atomic neutron element. . . ."

That's when I cut him off. "That's okay, Professor. You lost me at 'DEMOUSERATTO LOGARITHM.'"

The professor **smiled**. "Sorry about that! I get carried away sometimes!"

NOT THE RED BUTTON

The professor, Hercule Poirat, and I were so busy chatting, we forgot about *Count von Snootrat* for a minute. He saw his chance. Faster than a gazelle, he leapt toward the Voltometer. "If I can't use this machine, then no one else will be able to, either!" He grabbed the controls and pushed the red self-destruct button.

"NO! NOT THE RED BUTTON!" shrieked Professor von Volt.

The *VOLTOMETER* began to hum louder and louder . . .

BzzzzzzzzzzzzzzzzzzzzzzzZZZZ...

Then it began to smoke. There was a horrible stench of burned wires and metal.

Within a few moments, the machine had melted!

The professor sank to his knees next to the wreckage. "**Oh, no!** Building this **machine** was my life's work!" He buried his snout in his paws.

I wanted to **comfort** him, but I didn't know what to say. I imagined how I'd feel if all the books I'd ever written were destroyed. I'd be **devastated!**

Fortunately, **Professor Paws von Volt** recovered quickly. "Well, perhaps it's for the best," he said, sighing. "Like many of the best inventions, it proved to be **DANGEROUS** in the paws of an untrustworthy rat!"

I Can't Stand Bananas!

Once the news of Count von Snootrat's cheating got out, the competitions that he had won were voided. Then the events were repeated the next day. And this time, it was the best athletes who won, not the most SNEAKY.

There was a special ceremony to thank Hercule Poirat and me for solving the case. I was a little embarrassed by all the attention. But at the same time, I knew Grandfather would be proud when he heard the news.

"HURRAY FOR HERCULE POIRAT! HURRAY FOR GERONIMO STILTON!" all the athletes cheered.

Hercule took a bow. Then he shouted,

"Three cheers for all the athletes! Especially the ones from Mouse Island!"

That got a huge cheer from the audience. "HIP, HIP, HOORAY! HIP, HIP, HOORAY!"

Hercule sat down again and began chewing on a banana. "Would you like a banana, my dear Stilton? You see, this one is special because—"

I cut him off. I just couldn't bear to have this conversation again. "No, thank you!"

"Come on, just give it a little taste. You'll see why," Hercule continued.

"Thank you, but no," I said firmly.

"Try just a little bite," he insisted.

"I'm not hungry."

"But it's really a good banana. Just let me explain . . ."

"Not only do they upset my stomach, but also, I hate them!"

"But it would be impossible for you not to like this banana! If you'll just let me explain. . . ."

"I can't stand the taste of bananas!" I shouted. "I hate bananas! I despise them! I detest them! I loathe them!" I stopped at last . . . but only because I had run out of words that mean hate!

He waved a banana under my nose. "But my dear Stilton, these don't taste like

Sniff, sniff, sniff...

bananas! They taste like CHEESE! That's what I've been trying to tell you!"

I looked at him suspiciously. Then, cautiously, I leaned in to smell the banana.

Hercule was absolutely right! It was the tastiest banana I'd ever had.

In fact, it was scrumptious!

"This is not your everyday banana, Stilton," Hercule explained. "I soaked it in **melted cheese** all night. What do you think, my dear Stilton?"

Yum!

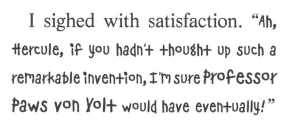

I sighed with satisfaction. "Ah, Hercule, if you hadn't thought up such a remarkable invention, I'm sure Professor Paws von Volt would have eventually!"

GERONIMO, YOU'RE AMAZING!

But the real surprise was still to come.

When the **Olympics** wrapped up, Hercule Poirat and I boarded the first plane back to New Mouse City. Despite what I'd told Thea and Grandfather, I was sad to leave Athens. It was truly a *beautiful* city, and one with so much fascinating history. I couldn't wait to come back for a visit.

After a **BUMPY** flight, Hercule and I *scrambled* off the plane together. It was good to be home.

Much to our surprise, there was a huge crowd of rodents waiting around at the airport.

"Geronimo, you're amaaaazing!

I turned **red** as a tomato. "Wh-wh-who, me?" I stuttered.

The crowd pushed down the barriers. More than a thousand female rodents rushed toward me.

It was terrifying! I scampered away as fast as I could.

"Run, my dear Stilton! Run!" called Hercule.

At that moment, my cell phone rang. It was my sister, Thea.

"Geronimo, your TV broadcasts of the **Olympics** were stupendous! By the way, you look great on TV. All my friends want to meet you. And what an adventure you had! It's the kind of thing that only happens to you and HERCULE POIRAT!"

Facts About the Modern Olympics

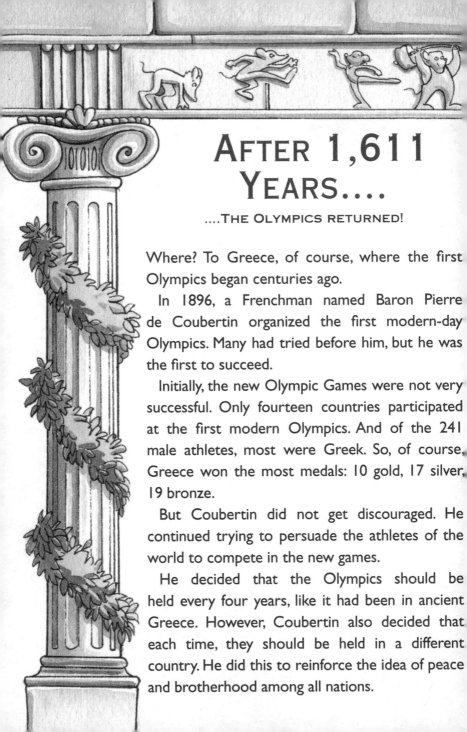

AFTER 1,611 YEARS....

....THE OLYMPICS RETURNED!

Where? To Greece, of course, where the first Olympics began centuries ago.

In 1896, a Frenchman named Baron Pierre de Coubertin organized the first modern-day Olympics. Many had tried before him, but he was the first to succeed.

Initially, the new Olympic Games were not very successful. Only fourteen countries participated at the first modern Olympics. And of the 241 male athletes, most were Greek. So, of course, Greece won the most medals: 10 gold, 17 silver, 19 bronze.

But Coubertin did not get discouraged. He continued trying to persuade the athletes of the world to compete in the new games.

He decided that the Olympics should be held every four years, like it had been in ancient Greece. However, Coubertin also decided that each time, they should be held in a different country. He did this to reinforce the idea of peace and brotherhood among all nations.

A REAL SUPER-DUPER ATHLETE!

"THE MOST IMPORTANT THING IN THE OLYMPIC GAMES IS NOT TO WIN BUT TO PARTICIPATE!"

This famous quote from Pierre de Coubertin (1863–1937) is the cornerstone of the modern Olympic Games.

Coubertin was an admirer of the ancient Greek world. He was firmly convinced that sport played an important role in developing the minds and bodies of young people. He also felt the Games could be the perfect tool for improving relations among different nations. And so in 1894, he proposed the rebirth of the Olympic Games to an international committee, which became the first International Olympic Committee.

Coubertin was named Honorary President of the Olympic Games. According to his wishes, his heart was buried in Olympia, Greece, in a monument commemorating the revival of the Olympic Games.

And so, with only a few interruptions, the Olympic Games have continued to this day. Surely, Coubertin would have been very pleased with his accomplishments. In 1896, only fourteen countries participated in Greece, and in 1948, after World War II, only fifty-nine countries participated in London. But by 2004, in Athens, 201 countries and 10,625 athletes competed in 301 events!

Many things have changed since the early Olympics. For example, at the Paris Games in 1900, all the swimming competitions took place in the Seine River...with the currents

always in the swimmers' favor! Today, of course, all the swimming competitions are held in special Olympic-size pools.

At the same Olympics, in Paris in 1900, winners were awarded umbrellas and books as their prizes, despite what Coubertin had requested be given as awards: a medal, a certificate, and a laurel branch in remembrance of the ancient games.

THE OATH

In the name of all the competitors, I promise that we shall take part in these Olympic Games, respecting and abiding by the rules which govern them, committing ourselves to a sport without doping and without drugs, in the true spirit of sportsmanship, for the glory of sport and the honor of our teams.

The Olympic Oath is taken by each athlete at the opening ceremonies of every games to emphasize the spirit that should be present during every competition.

IN THE SHADOW OF THE TORCH

The Olympic flame is a symbol of the spirit of brotherhood among all people. Every four years, a few months before the Games, a fire is lit near the ruins of an ancient temple in Olympia, Greece, using the sun and a mirror. A torch is ignited from this fire, and then a team of athletes from many different countries relay the flame to the place where the Olympics will take place that year. The athletes who carry the flame are called torchbearers.

The flame can be transported by bicycle, car, train, boat, or plane. Otherwise, it is passed from hand to hand by runners on foot every kilometer until it reaches the Olympic stadium in the host city. There it is used to light the cauldron that will burn for the duration of the Games. It is a great honor to be the final torchbearer, who is usually a citizen of the host country.

THE FIVE
OLYMPIC CIRCLES

Naturally, it was the father of the Olympic Games, Pierre de Coubertin, who thought of such a simple and clear symbol to represent the spirit of the Olympics. Once again, Coubertin found his inspiration in antiquity. When he was studying rituals from the ancient games, he saw five intertwined circles on an altar in Greece. These circles were used as a symbol of truce during the Delphic games. Coubertin thought they would be the perfect representation of the five continents on our planet.

The circles on the white background have at least one color from all the flags of the world. Every circle corresponds to a continent: yellow for Asia; black for Africa; blue for Europe; red for the Americas; and green for Oceania.

At the end of each Games, the Olympic flag is given to the country that will host the next Olympics.

The first Olympic flag made its debut in 1920 at the games held in Antwerp, Belgium. But that was not the only new aspect of the seventh modern Olympics.

Women in the Olympics

During ancient times, women could not participate or even attend the Olympic Games. At the first modern Olympics in 1896, things were not much different. Obviously, women could attend the Games, but they did not compete until 1900 in Paris in tennis and croquet. Out of 997 athletes, only 22 were women. Now, one of the goals of the Olympics is to promote women in sport at all levels. Out of 10,624 athletes in the 2004 Summer Olympics, 4,329 were women!

THE CHRONOMETER

The first quartz electronic chronometer made its appearance during the Games in Tokyo, Japan, in 1964. Before then, time was measured with a mechanical chronometer. In those early competitions, it was not easy to establish the winner — especially in the swimming or track competitions, when the advantage could come down to a hundredth of a second.

In case of a tie, a decision was made by the judges, who were not always in agreement. Today's technology allows the judges to immediately evaluate the results to a thousandth of a second. In fact, with the aid of photo imaging, the judges can watch athletes cross the finish line on a computer monitor that shows them each competitor's time directly underneath his or her picture.

THE SUMMER OLYMPICS

When people talk about the Olympics, everyone immediately thinks of the Summer Games that take place every four years. The Summer Olympics has the most competitions: more than three hundred individual and team events. These are also the games in which the greatest number of athletes participate: More than 10,000 athletes participated in the Summer Olympics held in Athens in 2004.

One reason the Summer Games are so huge is that every sport includes specialized disciplines or events. For example, the swimming competition is broken up into several events, including diving, synchronized swimming, and water polo.

Field events include three disciplines: running, jumping, and throwing. These three disciplines include many individual and team events. Just think of how many track competitions there are: starting from the 100-meter dash, which lasts only a few seconds, to the marathon, which is more than twenty-six miles long and lasts hours!

THE WINTER OLYMPICS

In 1924, the seventh Olympic Summer Games were held in Paris, France, while the first Olympic Winter Games took place in Chamonix, France. Until 1990, both the Winter and Summer Games were held in the same year.

After the 1990 Games, it was decided to reschedule the Summer and Winter Games by alternating between them, so that the Olympics would take place every two years. Each would still be held in a four-year cycle, but two years apart from each other.

Organizing the first Winter Games was not easy, even though there were fewer athletes and events than in the Summer Games.

Why? The problem, first and foremost, was the snow! Today, we have machines that can make artificial snow, but not back then. During the 1964 Winter Games in Innsbruck, Austria the Austrian Army had to bring in tons of snow and ice by truck because it had not yet snowed!

The Winter Games have more than eighty events. The individual and team competitions are in the following sports: biathlon, bobsled, curling, ice hockey, luge, skating, and skiing.

WHAT ARE THE PARALYMPICS?

An English doctor named Sir Ludwig Guttman had the idea of starting a sports competition as part of the rehabilitation process for handicapped war veterans. The first games took place in Stoke Mandeville, England, at the same time the Olympic Games were going on in London, in 1948. His event was so successful that after a short time, these games became international. During the Summer Paralympic Games in Rome in 1960, four hundred mentally and physically challenged athletes from twenty-three different nations participated. Close to four thousand athletes from 136 countries took part in the 2004 Paralympic Summer Games in Athens, competing in nineteen different events.

Since the 1988 Summer Olympics in Seoul and the 1992 Winter Olympics in Albertville, disabled athletes were able to compete using the same venues as the Olympic competitors. That's how the games got the name Paralympics — that is, games that take place parallel to the Olympics.

Summer sports include archery, cycling, swimming, volleyball, and weightlifting. Winter sports include alpine and cross-country skiing, ice hockey, and wheelchair curling.

SPORTS THAT COME AND GO

Did you know that in 1920 tug-of-war was an Olympic sport? That rugby was an Olympic sport for a few years, and then was taken off the program? That tennis was added, then scrapped, then reinstated? That the last summer sport to make a debut was tae kwon do? That snowboarding is now a Winter Olympic event?

Who decides which sport to include and which to exclude?

In the past, there was a lot of confusion as to what sports were to be included. It was up to the host country to decide which events were to be included and which were to be excluded. The decision was based on their preferences and their local cultural traditions. Since this was not exactly a fair criterion, the practice gave rise to a lot of criticism.

And so the Olympic Committee came up with a rule that was fair for everyone. For male athletes, the sport needed to be played in seventy-five countries and four continents. For women, a given sport needed to be played in forty countries and three continents. This way, there would be no favoritism and all could participate, at least in theory, with the same chance of winning.

THE BIATHLON

What is the biathlon? It is a race that combines cross-country skiing with rifle shooting. Biathlon competitors ski a long-distance race, stopping every so often to shoot at a target along the course. The winner not only must complete the race in the shortest time possible but must also have the best target shooting.

AMATEURS OR PROFESSIONALS?

At the first modern Olympics, it was decided that athletes must be amateurs—that is, they could not receive any money for playing or have any sponsors. Since sport federations were not yet in existence, the only athletes who could compete were those who had the means to do so. It was a very strict rule. An Italian athlete fell victim to it when he was denied participation at the first Olympic Games in Athens. Jim Thorpe was stripped of his decathlon and pentathlon medals from the 1912 Olympics because he had been paid two dollars a game for playing minor league baseball.

Today, even professional athletes are allowed to compete. At the Olympic Games, it is now possible to see the best athletes in the world. Winning an Olympic gold medal is the highest aspiration for athletes in every nation!

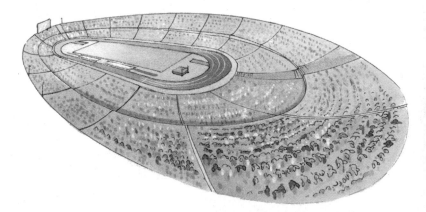

THE OLYMPIC VILLAGE

In ancient Olympia, there were no real accommodations for athletes. Since all sports were religious in nature, competitions were held in temples.

The first time all the athletes and their teams were accommodated in an Olympic Village was in 1924 in Paris. The "village" was a group of wood cabins.

With the number of participating nations and athletes constantly on the rise, the size of the Olympic Village has also increased. The Olympic Village at the 2004 games in Athens housed 24,000 people, including the athletes and their coaches and trainers. Each day, 50,000 meals were served, using 100 tons of food.

GREAT OLYMPIC ATHLETES

JESSE OWENS: At the 1936 Olympics in Berlin, the American track athlete Jesse Owens won a gold medal in the 100-meter dash, the 200-meter dash, long jump, and 4 x 100-meter relay. He set two Olympic records and a world record.

TANNI GREY-THOMPSON: One of the most famous Paralympics champions. This British athlete has won fourteen medals in all, nine of which are gold. In the 1992 games in Barcelona, she won four gold medals, including one for the 400-meter race.

CARL LEWIS: At the 1984 Los Angeles Olympics, the American runner Carl Lewis won the gold in the 100-meter dash, the 200-meter dash, the long jump, and the 4 x 100-meter relay, tying Jesse Owens's record.

NADIA COMANECI: At the 1976 Olympics in Montreal, at barely fourteen years of age, Romanian gymnast Nadia Comaneci won three gold medals, a silver medal, and a bronze medal. She was the first athlete to score a perfect 10.0 on the uneven parallel bars.

MARK SPITZ: At the 1972 Summer Games in Monaco, the American swimmer Mark Spitz won a record-setting seven gold medals — for the 100-meter freestyle, the 200-meter freestyle, the 100-meter butterfly, the 200-meter butterfly, the 1 x 400-meter freestyle relay, the 4 x 200-meter freestyle relay, and the 4 x 100-meter medley relay. Over a period of eight days, Spitz won seven Olympic events and set a world record at every single one.

JEAN-CLAUDE KILLY: At the 1968 Winter Olympics in Grenoble, this French athlete won three gold medals in alpine skiing (downhill, slalom, and giant slalom).

KATARINA WITT: At the 1988 Winter Olympics in Calgary, this German athlete noted for her remarkable grace on the ice won a gold medal in women's figure skating for the second consecutive time.

RAISA SMETANINA: In the five Olympics held between 1976 and 1992, this Russian skier won a total of four golds, five silvers, and one bronze. She holds the record for most medals — ten in all — won by a female athlete in the Olympic Games.

OLYMPIC RECORDS!

SOCCER: The countries that have won the most Olympic medals in soccer are Great Britain (1900, 1908, and 1912) and Hungary (1952, 1964, and 1968) — three each.

VOLLEYBALL: This sport was introduced in 1964 as an Olympic event for both men and women. The former Soviet Union has brought home the most gold medals in this event, both for men (in 1964, 1968, and 1980) and women (in 1968, 1972, 1980, and 1988).

TABLE TENNIS (Ping-Pong): The record for the most gold medals belongs to Deng Yaping of China, who won four titles total in singles and doubles in 1992 and 1996.

TRACK: The American Ray Ewry holds the record for the most gold medals won by a male athlete, with ten in all for the high jump, long jump, and triple jump (in 1900, 1904, 1906, and 1908). Among female athletes, Fanny Blankers-Koen (Holland), Betty Cuthbert

(Australia), Barbel Wöckel-Eckert (German Democratic Republic), and Evelyn Ashford (USA) are tied for the most golds, with four each.

COUNTRIES WITH GREATEST PARTICIPATION: Since 1896 only five nations have always participated in the Olympics: Australia, France, Greece, Great Britain, and Switzerland.

MOST GOLD MEDALS WON BY A COUNTRY: From 1896 to 2006, the United States has won the most gold medals: 943.

MOST ATHLETES IN A SINGLE OLYMPIC GAMES: In the 2004 Olympic Games in Athens, Greece, 10,625 competed, of which 4,329 were women — also a record number.

Want to read my next adventure?
It's sure to be a fur-raising experience!

GERONIMO STILTON, SECRET AGENT

My sister, Thea, is the mystery-loving rodent, not me! But somehow I found myself going undercover to get to the bottom of a case. Slimy Swiss balls—I hardly knew where to start! Geronimo Stilton, Secret Agent Mouse? Maybe I could get used to that....

And don't miss any of my other fabumouse adventures!

 #1 Lost Treasure of the Emerald Eye

 #2 The Curse of the Cheese Pyramid

 #3 Cat and Mouse in a Haunted House

 #4 I'm Too Fond of My Fur!

 #5 Four Mice Deep in the Jungle

 #6 Paws Off, Cheddarface!

 #7 Red Pizzas for a Blue Count

 #8 Attack of the Bandit Cats

 #9 A Fabumouse Vacation for Geronimo

 #10 All Because of a Cup of Coffee

 #11 It's Halloween, You 'Fraidy Mouse!

 #12 Merry Christmas, Geronimo!

#13 The Phantom of the Subway

#14 The Temple of the Ruby of Fire

#15 The Mona Mousa Code

#16 A Cheese-Colored Campe

#17 Watch Your Whiskers, Stilton!

#18 Shipwreck on the Pirate Islands

#19 My Name Is Stilton, Geronimo Stilton

#20 Surf's Up, Geronimo!

#21 The Wild, Wild West

#22 The Secret of Cacklefur Castle

A Christmas Tale

#23 Valentine's Day Disaster

#24 Field Trip to Niagara Falls

#25 The Search for Sunken Treasure

#26 The Mummy with No Name

#27 The Christmas Toy Factory

#28 Wedding Crasher

#29 Down and Out Down Under

#30 The Mouse Island Marathon

#31 The Mysterious Cheese Thief

Christmas Catastrophe

#32 Valley of the Giant Skeletons

and coming soon

#34 Geronimo Stilton, Secret Agent

ABOUT THE AUTHOR

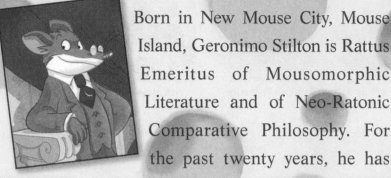

Born in New Mouse City, Mouse Island, Geronimo Stilton is Rattus Emeritus of Mousomorphic Literature and of Neo-Ratonic Comparative Philosophy. For the past twenty years, he has been running *The Rodent's Gazette,* New Mouse City's most widely read daily newspaper.

Stilton was awarded the Ratitzer Prize for his scoops on *The Curse of the Cheese Pyramid* and *The Search for Sunken Treasure.* He has also received the Andersen 2000 Prize for Personality of the Year. One of his bestsellers won the 2002 eBook Award for world's best ratlings' electronic book. His works have been published all over the globe.

In his spare time, Mr. Stilton collects antique cheese rinds and plays golf. But what he most enjoys is telling stories to his nephew Benjamin.

THE RODENT'S GAZETTE

1. **Main entrance**
2. **Printing presses (where the books and newspaper are printed)**
3. **Accounts department**
4. **Editorial room (where the editors, illustrators, and designers work)**
5. **Geronimo Stilton's office**
6. **Storage space for Geronimo's books**

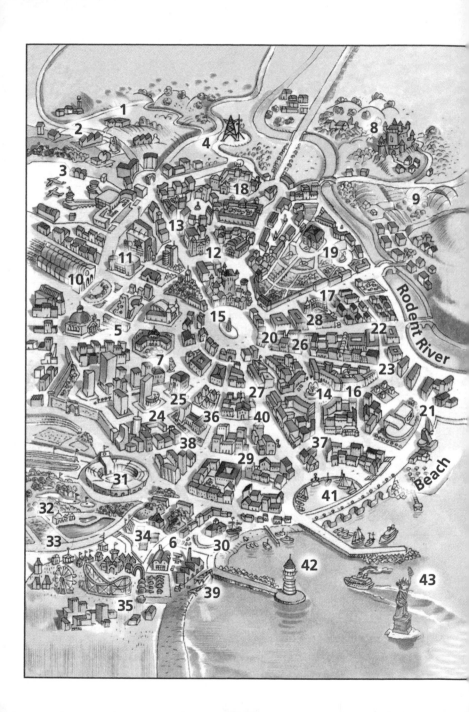

Map of New Mouse City

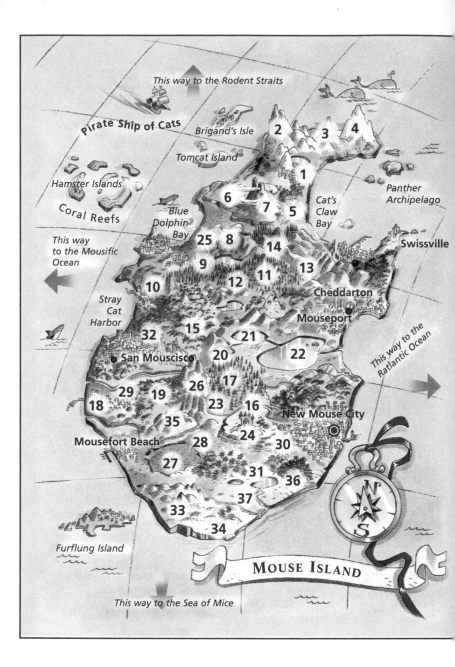

Map of Mouse Island

Dear mouse friends,
Thanks for reading, and farewell
till the next book.
It'll be another whisker-licking-good
adventure, and that's a promise!

Geronimo Stilton